JOURNEY
to the
MOON

Caroline Rose
Illustrations by Mike Dorey

BARRON'S

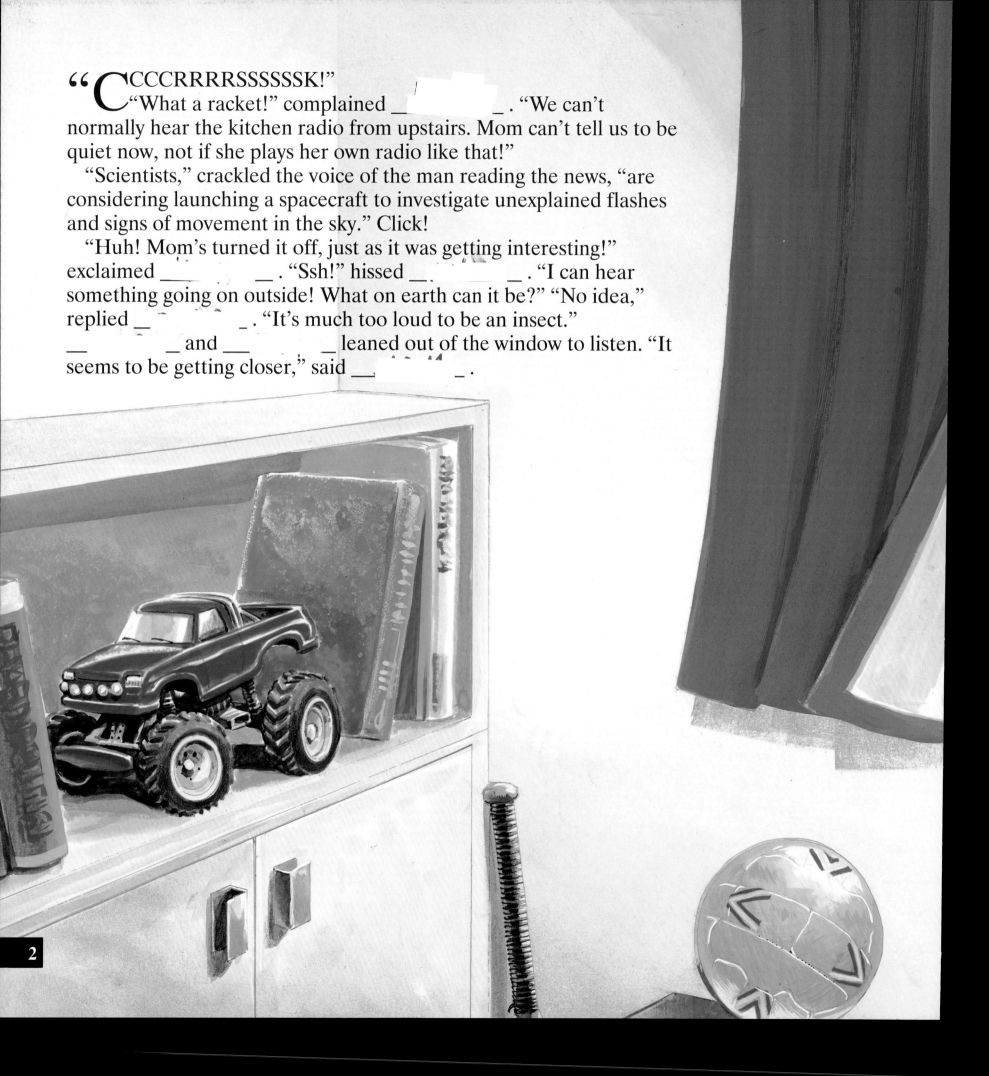

"CCCCRRRRSSSSSSK!"

"What a racket!" complained _____. "We can't normally hear the kitchen radio from upstairs. Mom can't tell us to be quiet now, not if she plays her own radio like that!"

"Scientists," crackled the voice of the man reading the news, "are considering launching a spacecraft to investigate unexplained flashes and signs of movement in the sky." Click!

"Huh! Mom's turned it off, just as it was getting interesting!" exclaimed _____. "Ssh!" hissed _____. "I can hear something going on outside! What on earth can it be?" "No idea," replied _____. "It's much too loud to be an insect."

_____ and _____ leaned out of the window to listen. "It seems to be getting closer," said _____.

"There's something very odd happening to that circle of grass over there. It's glowing!" "It's gone flat, too," added _____.

As _____ and _____ stared, the glow mysteriously began to fade.

"It's gone now," said _____. "Mom's just turned out the kitchen light. I think we must have been imagining things," remarked

_____. "We probably were. It's a pity, though. I'd love to have an adventure."

"Maybe we will," laughed _____, "because I can hear something else! And I think it's coming this way!"

_____ and _____ were now aware of a scratching sound. Someone, or something, was scrambling up the side of the house. _____ and _____ peered down into the darkness.

"Don't lean out so far!" warned _____ , tugging _____ back into the room. "You'll fall!" "You didn't have to pull so hard," said _____ , breathlessly. "I'd swear I touched something alive. Oh no! It's coming in! Look! The curtains are moving!"

"It's only the wind," began _____ , before stopping abruptly. After all, both knew that the night was a calm one.

Otherwise, they would not have heard the movements up the side of the house. Nor would they have heard another strange sound—a tiny hiss, just like a bottle of soda being opened. Suddenly, it was as if the hiss had started to shine. _____ and _____ watched in amazement.

There it was, twisting and weaving color as it whirled around two mysterious shapes.

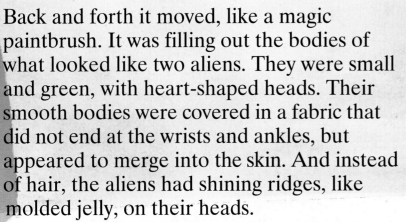

Back and forth it moved, like a magic paintbrush. It was filling out the bodies of what looked like two aliens. They were small and green, with heart-shaped heads. Their smooth bodies were covered in a fabric that did not end at the wrists and ankles, but appeared to merge into the skin. And instead of hair, the aliens had shining ridges, like molded jelly, on their heads.

"It looks as if you could eat their hair! I bet it tastes like spinach!" thought _____ .

One alien was holding something like a gun. A trace of shining gas was still rising from its barrel, slowly making the lower limbs of the alien forms visible.

"I'd love to know what that funny-looking box on that one's wrist is. Do you think they'd tell us?" "Only if they could hear us ask. But they don't seem to have any ears." "Maybe they'll hear if we shout loudly enough," suggested _____ . But the aliens were making urgent signs to _____ and _____ to be quiet.

At first, the aliens spoke so quietly that _____ and _____ had to lean close to hear them. "I think the sound's coming out of that wrist box," remarked _____ . "It's no good, though. I still can't understand what they're saying. It's a very funny language."

"Ozh dezar!" said one of the aliens desperately. "Trzy! Yozu muzst trzy harzder!" "I've got it!" cried _____ , suddenly. "It *is* English after all! It's just that every word has a Z in the middle! It's like a secret code." The aliens waved their arms about.

"Quizck!" they said. "Wze hazve az lozt tzo dzo. Anzd nzo, _____ , wze dzo nozt eazt ouzr hazir, anzd izt doeszn't taszte lizke spiznach." _____ blushed. "What's that about eating their hair because it tastes like spinach?" asked _____ , completely bewildered.

"Izt mezans," said the alien, "thzat ozn Plaznet Earzth, yozu hazve tzo usze worzds. Mandzria, whezre wze cozme frzom, izs mozre advaznced. Wze hazve eazrs undzer thze skzin, lizke fizsh ozr snazkes dzo, buzt wze dozn't usze thzem fozr converzsation. Everzyone spezaks strazight inzto eazch othzer's miznds."

"I get it," said _____ , still very red. "They can hear what we're thinking, but we can't hear them without that wrist box."

_____ tried to think nice thoughts. The aliens laughed. "So you're not going to kill us?" asked _____ . "Nzo!" said the aliens. "Wze arze frieznds. Buzt hurrzy!" "How do we know we can trust you?" asked _____ . "We can't hear *your* thoughts."

"Okzay. Thzen wze muszt hazve nzo secrzets," agreed the aliens. "Firzst, _____ wouzld lizke tzo knzow hozw thze speezch bozx worzks. It'zs vezry simzple. Izt puzts ouzr thouzghts inzto whatzever langzuage thze listzener wizll underzstand. Izt izs nozt perfzect, thouzgh, becazuse wze hazd szo littzle tizme bezfore wze cazme."

The aliens let _____ press the button that opened the box. _____ and _____ had never seen anything like it. They couldn't understand how it worked, but they admired the aliens for having invented such an extraordinary thing. They must be incredibly advanced on Mandria. But if so, why had the aliens come to Planet Earth? Why did they seem in such a hurry? And what did they want with _____ and _____ ?

"Tizme izs shozrt," said one of the aliens. "Yozu muzst liszten vezry carefzully tzo whzat wze hazve tzo tezll yozu."

"Thezre arze mazny inhabzited planzets," explained the taller alien, "buzt thzey arze furtzher awzay thzan youzr scienztists cazn imagzine."

"How wonderful!" sighed _____ . "I'd love to visit Mandria. Then I'd go to all the other planets afterward!" "Yozu wouzld nozt," replied the other alien sadly. "Thzat izs whzy wze arze hezre. Yozu szee, nozt alzl thze planzets hazve uszed thezir knowlzedge wezll," he continued. "Izn sozme, greezd anzd luzst fozr powzer izs alzl thzat mattzers. Thzey mazde weazpons tzo figzht agaiznst eaczh othzer. Thze fighzting thezn sprezad untizll mazny planzets wezre azt wazr."

"How terrifying!" exclaimed _____ . "Yezs," said the alien. "Izt wazs. Thze peaczeful planzets wezre izn grezat danzger. Szo thze B-9 Forzce wazs forzmed."

"The what?" asked _____ . "Uzs! Anzd othzers lizke uzs," chorused the aliens.

"We'zre azn intergazlactic peazcekeepzing forzce, drazwn frzom planzets lizke Mandzria, thazt arze nozt azt wazr. Lozok whzat yozu wizll lozse withzout ouzr hezlp."

One of the aliens now produced a small case. In it was a tiny picture. Wonder of wonders, he made the picture stretch until it covered one whole wall. The image seemed to be alive and moving. Whales leaped in the ocean so that _____ and _____ ducked instinctively, to avoid being soaked by the spray.

"It's a sort of hologram!" exclaimed _____ , trying to touch one of the waves with a finger. "It's dry, but it feels as if you could walk right into it."

"Withzout yozur hezlp, alzl thezse lovzely thizngs wizll dize," warned one of the aliens, as he put this picture back in its case.

Next the aliens showed _____ and _____ a hologram of a very different place. The land was scarred, and great areas were covered with filthy smoke.

"Where on earth is that?" asked _____ in horror.

"Fortunzately, izt izs nozt ozn Earzth, buzt izf wze dzo nozt hurrzy, thzat izs hozw thze Earzth wizll beczome," said one of the aliens. "Thzis izs az planzet callzed D-Skrozid."

"D-Skroid? What a horrible place!" shuddered _____ . As they looked into the picture, two hideous figures appeared from behind a broken wall. Their red skin was covered in sores, and they looked half starved. These vile creatures hurled weapons at each other's heads. Then they leaped at each other, snarling and slashing like animals, with their filthy claws.

"Stop them!" begged _____ , as the alien put the hologram back into its case.

"Thezse monszters arze thze Skroizds," said one of the aliens. "Izf yozu dzo nozt hezlp thze B-9 Forzce, thze Skroizds wizll tazke ovzer yozur planzet, tozo."

"Ugh! But why do the Skroids want Planet Earth?" gasped _____ .

"Greezd." said an alien. "Thezir owzn planzet is almzost deazd. Earzth wouzld suizt thzem vezry wezll."

"We must stop them!" cried _____ .

"Yozur primiztive weapzons arze nzo usze agaiznst thze Skroizds," the alien continued. "Yozur protezction agaiznst invazders uszed tzo bze youzr ozozne layzer, befzore peozple ozn Earzth began releazsing szo mazny chemizcals inzto thezir atmoszphere. Thze Skroizds cazn gezt izn throuzgh thze holzes thzat chemizcals hazve mazde."

"We'd do anything to save planet Earth!" said _____ .

"Thezn yozu muzst cozme wizth uzs ozn az jourzney."

"Thze futzure ozf thze worzld izs izn yozur hanzds," said one of the aliens. "Onzly yozu cazn dzo thze jozb," he announced. "Quiczkly! gezt dresszed anzd cozme wizth uzs."

"We'd better stuff sweaters into our beds to make it look as if we're asleep," said _____ . "Otherwise Mom will have the police out looking for us!" laughed _____ . "Goozd thinzking!" said an alien.

Once _____ and _____ were ready, the other alien took out the vapor gun, made both himself and his friend invisible, and then aimed it at _____ and _____ . "You've got a hole straight through your middle!" exclaimed _____ .

"You've only got one leg, but two feet."

More vapor swirled around the room. Suddenly, they heard footsteps. Mom looked around the door. "Oh!" she said. "They're asleep already. I could have sworn I heard voices!"

_____ and _____ put invisible hands over their mouths to silence their giggles, and Mom crept quietly downstairs.

"You'zre stanzding ozn mzy foozt," said the voice of an alien. "Sorry! Anyway, someone has his elbow in my ear!" complained _____ . "Staznd stizll, anzd Iz'll liznk everzyone's hanzds togezther szo nzo onze gezts lozst ozn thze wazy tzo thze spacezship. It'zs inviszible, tzoo. Lezt's azll tipztoe downsztairs."

"I wonder if it's in the yard where the grass has gone flat?" thought _____ .

As _____ and _____ entered the spaceship, together with the aliens, they passed through rays that made them all visible once again. They could also now see the inside of the craft. There were no gleaming dials or flashing lights, simply a panel that responded to orders given with their minds.

"Wze wizll explzain ozn thze jourzney. Strzap yourszelves izn fozr takzeofzf. Wze arze ofzf tzo thze Moozn."

_____ and _____ were aware of odd feelings in their tummies as the spaceship lifted off the ground. Through the window, the glowing Moon grew rapidly larger.

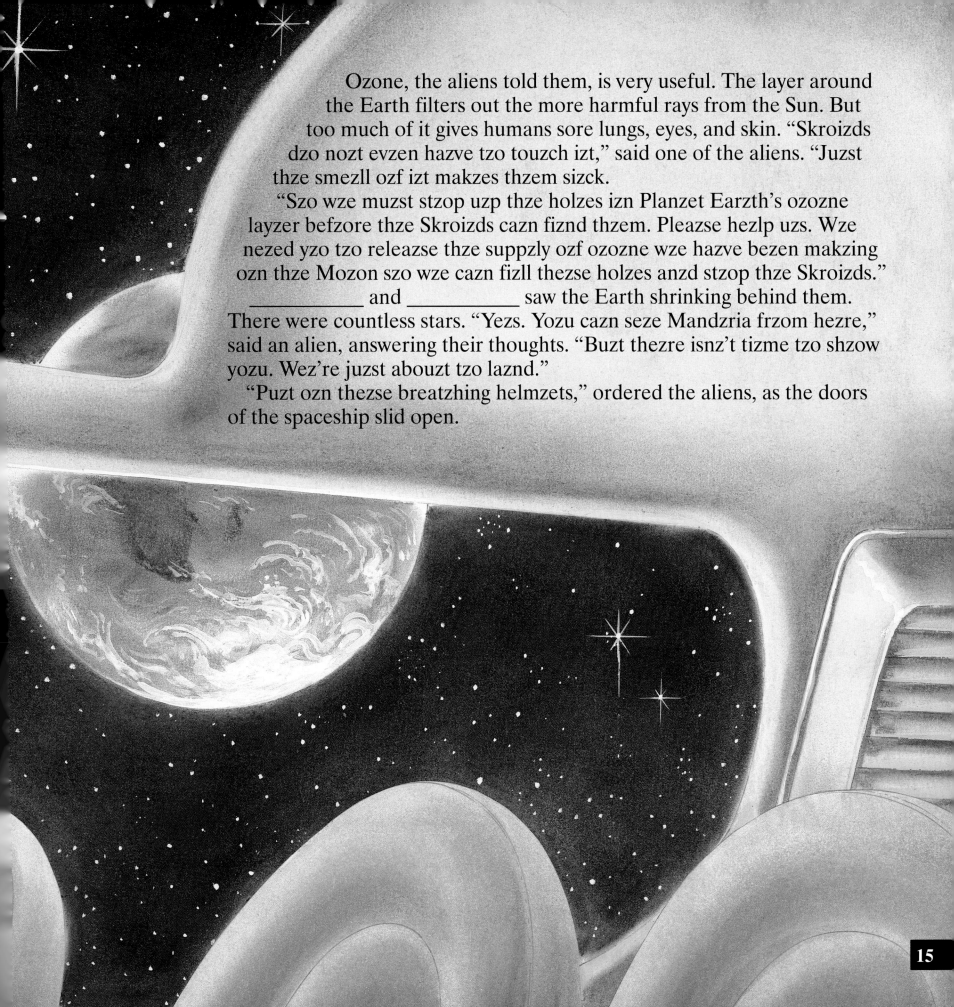

Ozone, the aliens told them, is very useful. The layer around the Earth filters out the more harmful rays from the Sun. But too much of it gives humans sore lungs, eyes, and skin. "Skroizds dzo nozt evzen hazve tzo touzch izt," said one of the aliens. "Juzst thze smezll ozf izt makzes thzem sizck.

"Szo wze muzst stzop uzp thze holzes izn Planzet Earzth's ozozne layzer befzore thze Skroizds cazn fiznd thzem. Pleazse hezlp uzs. Wze nezed yzo tzo releazse thze suppzly ozf ozozne wze hazve bezen makzing ozn thze Mozon szo wze cazn fizll thezse holzes anzd stzop thze Skroizds." _____ and _____ saw the Earth shrinking behind them. There were countless stars. "Yezs. Yozu cazn seze Mandzria frzom hezre," said an alien, answering their thoughts. "Buzt thezre isnz't tizme tzo shzow yozu. Wez're juzst abouzt tzo laznd."

"Puzt ozn thezse breatzhing helmzets," ordered the aliens, as the doors of the spaceship slid open.

_____ and _____ gazed in wonder at the lunar landscape. It was amazing! There was no mist in the dry atmosphere, and they could see for miles. They leaped for joy, and shot high above the ground.

"We weigh almost nothing here!" crowed _____ . "It's the low gravity!" "I'm going to jump over you!" called _____ , and did. "I can jump further than that!" boasted _____ . Forgetting everything else, they leaped and tumbled on the Moon, counting how many somersaults they could turn before they hit the ground.

"Race you back to the spaceship!" yelled _____ . "But where is it?" asked _____ in alarm. "Oh, no!" said _____ miserably. "They've made it invisible again, probably so that the Skroids can't see it."

Carefully, they tried to retrace their steps toward where they guessed that the spaceship lay. Several times they got it wrong. Once, when they thought they must be getting close, they came upon a group of figures lying on stretchers . . . only they didn't look like the aliens that _____ and _____ knew.

These aliens looked almost
lifeless. Their once gleaming
skin was blotched with white
patches, and their eyes were red
and sore. Several other aliens, not much healthier,
were busy taking care of them.

"Thzat izs whzy wze neezd youzr hezlp," said a familiar
voice behind them. "Ozozne izs dangezrous fozr uzs azs wezll." "Will
they die?" asked _____ in horror. "Nozt izf thzey gezt bazck
tzo Mandzria izn tizme," was the reply.

"Show us what to do," said _____ . The aliens now led them
to the mouth of a huge crater. "Yozu muzst gzo dozwn thezre," they
said. "Wze cannzot follzow. Tazke thze speezch bozx, szo
wze cazn commzunicate. Buzt bze carezful wizth izt, itz's
thze onzly onze wze hazve."

_____ and _____ took one last look at
the surface of the Moon. Then they turned, and went
down the steps.

17

The crater was clean and well lit. "I still wonder why they chose us," said _____ as they went down.

It was in this very crater, the aliens told them, that the B-9 Force scientists had worked, mixing vital chemicals into huge vats behind a safety barrier. They then had to run electricity through the vats to make the mixture work, switching on the current as they fled. This had made ozone, in the form of safer, concentrated pellets. No one had been back since.

"Nozw wze neezd yozur breazth tzo actizvate thze pellzets inzto gazs. Humzan breazth hazs juzst thze rigzht amouznt ozf moiszture fozr thizs."

By now, _____ and _____ had reached what looked like a safety barrier. They opened it and passed through. What a huge hall! And what enormous vats!

"It'zs okzay. Thze electrzicity izs offz. Itz's sazfe to touzch thzem," said an alien. _____ and _____ opened a vat. Inside lay the pellets. They were deep blue.

"Seze thozse twzo shozvels bzy thze wazll!" said an alien. "Yozu muzst usze thzem tzo pzut thze pellzets inzto thze boxzes carefzully, anzd carrzy thzem tzo thze mouzth ozf thze cratzers szo thzat thze B-9 Forzce cazn lozad thzem onzto thze shzip,"
ordered the aliens.

"I wonder what those balloons over there are for," said _____ . "This is no place to have a party!" 'Thze ballzoons muzst bze loazded onzto thze spacezship wizth thze pellzets," said the voice.

_____ and _____ worked quickly. Soon the last pellet was packed, and the boxes were passed with the balloons to the aliens above. The remaining B-9 Force stood in a group to say good-bye. One of the aliens gave _____ and _____ some cakes. "Eat them," said the alien. "Theyz're mazde ozf bazrm whizch grozws ozn azll thze livzing planzets exczept Planzet Earzth. Bazrm hazs mazny wondezrful propezrties. Yozu mazy neezd thzem."

_____ and _____ gobbled down the cakes on the way to the spaceship. They were not that delicious, but they thought it would be rude to spit them out.

_____ and _____ watched the Earth draw near. Its blues and greens, and whirls of cloud, seemed more beautiful than ever. The spaceship orbited, and slowed down over shining snow.

"Thzis izs Antarzctica. Thze biggzest hozle izs hezre," said an alien. "Itz's nozt azll thze fauzlt ozf Mazn. Thze weatzher dozes ozozne damzage azs wezll." Far away they could see the movement of the Skroids's ships.

"Izf yozu fizll thze hozle ovzer Antarzctica, thze ozozne wizll sprzead ouzt lizke watzer, anzd fizll thze smazller holzes azs wezll. Buzt hurrzy! Eazch ozf yozu muzst tazke az ballzoon," continued the aliens. "Puzt thezse glozves ozn, plazce az pellzet inzto eazch ballzoon, anzd thzen blzow izt uzp. Izt wizll seazl itszelf. Nezxt, puzt thze ballzoons inzto thze aizr lozck, anzd shzut thze doozr behzind thzem. Waizt fozr thze lozck tzo puzmp itzs aizr bazck inzto thze spacezship, anzd releazse eazch ballzoon befzore yozu prepzare thze nezxt onze."

"Why not just open a window and let them go?" asked _____ . "It would be much quicker." "If we opened a window, we'd all be sucked out!" replied _____ .

The first balloon exploded into space. Gleaming blue vapor burst from it. It spread, gradually thinning until it vanished. "There's masses of ozone in each pellet!" shouted _____ . "Wze neezd izt! Thezre's masszes ozf spazce tzo bze fillzed," commented the aliens.

So _____ and _____ filled, and blew, and filled and blew. There was no time to look around or chat. The aliens made no sound.

_____ and _____ were too busy to wonder why. They had forgotten what happened to aliens when they came near ozone.

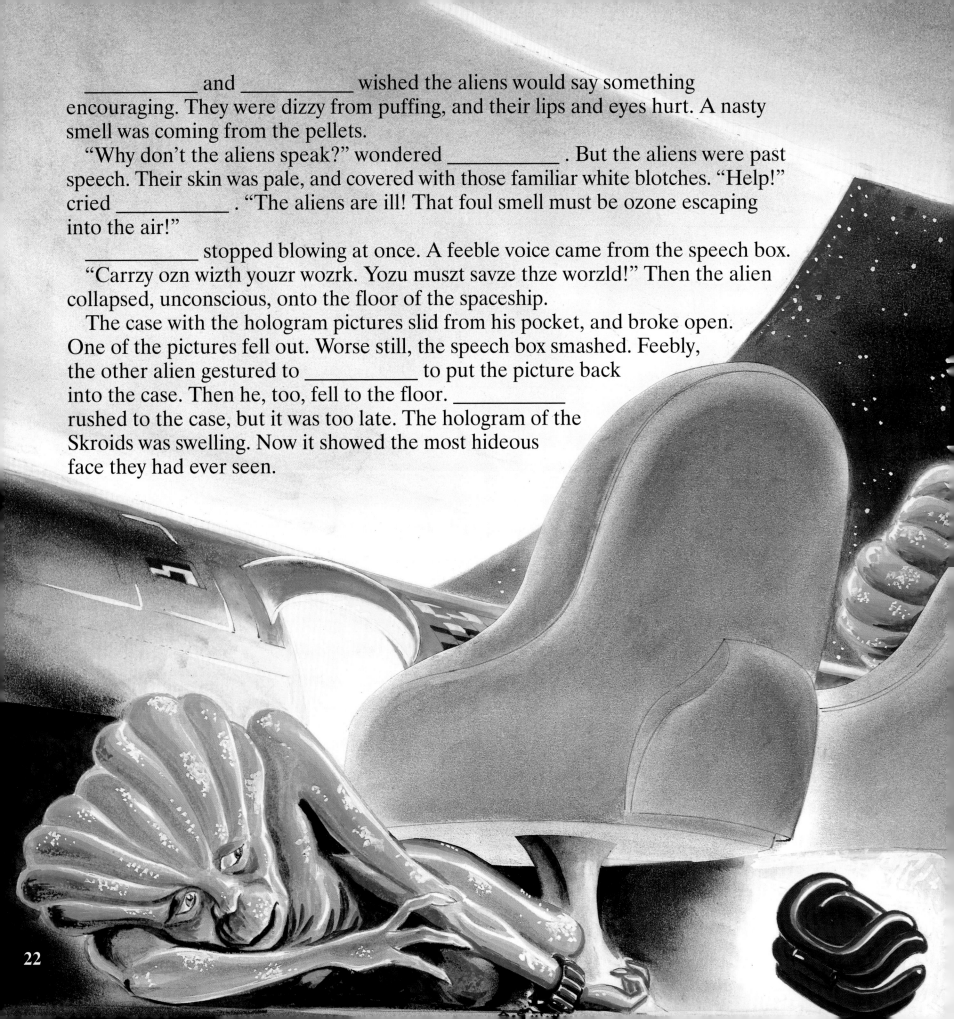

_____ and _____ wished the aliens would say something encouraging. They were dizzy from puffing, and their lips and eyes hurt. A nasty smell was coming from the pellets.

"Why don't the aliens speak?" wondered _____ . But the aliens were past speech. Their skin was pale, and covered with those familiar white blotches. "Help!" cried _____ . "The aliens are ill! That foul smell must be ozone escaping into the air!"

_____ stopped blowing at once. A feeble voice came from the speech box. "Carrzy ozn wizth youzr wozrk. Yozu muszt savze thze worzld!" Then the alien collapsed, unconscious, onto the floor of the spaceship.

The case with the hologram pictures slid from his pocket, and broke open. One of the pictures fell out. Worse still, the speech box smashed. Feebly, the other alien gestured to _____ to put the picture back into the case. Then he, too, fell to the floor. _____ rushed to the case, but it was too late. The hologram of the Skroids was swelling. Now it showed the most hideous face they had ever seen.

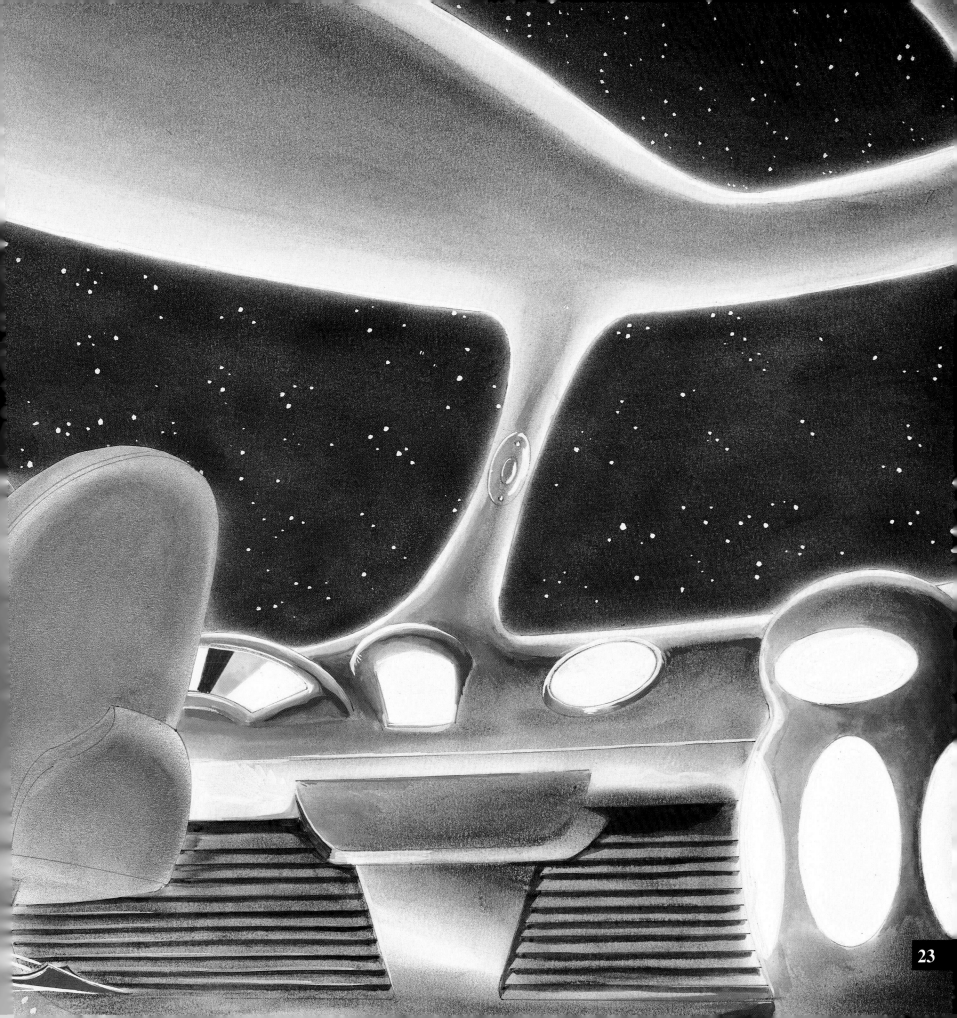

23

_____ and _____ were caught in the stare of the Skroid. Mercilessly, it sucked in everything they knew by reading their minds.
Desperately they struggled to resist.

"NO! This must not happen!" cried _____ , trying hard to close all thoughts against the probing eyes.

Out in space, the Skroids's spaceship had turned toward them. The Skroids could not see the B-9 Force craft, but they knew it was there because of the blue gas. And they were determined to reach Planet Earth before the holes in the ozone were filled.

A voice hissed from the hologram. "Yozu'll nevzer bezat mze! Arze yozu nozt surprzised Iz cazn tazlk? Iz toozk thze knowzledge frzom thze brozken speezch bozx."

"I HATE YOU!" _____ screamed in fury. "I think that's what it wants you to do," said _____ quietly. "Hating makes you become like a Skroid. Try to concentrate on the balloons, instead."

"Yozu'll nevzer gezt izt dozne izn tizme," sneered the Skroid. "Anyzway, thiznk hozw riczhly Iz wizll rewzard yozu izf yozu hezlp mze wizn Planzet Earzth."

25

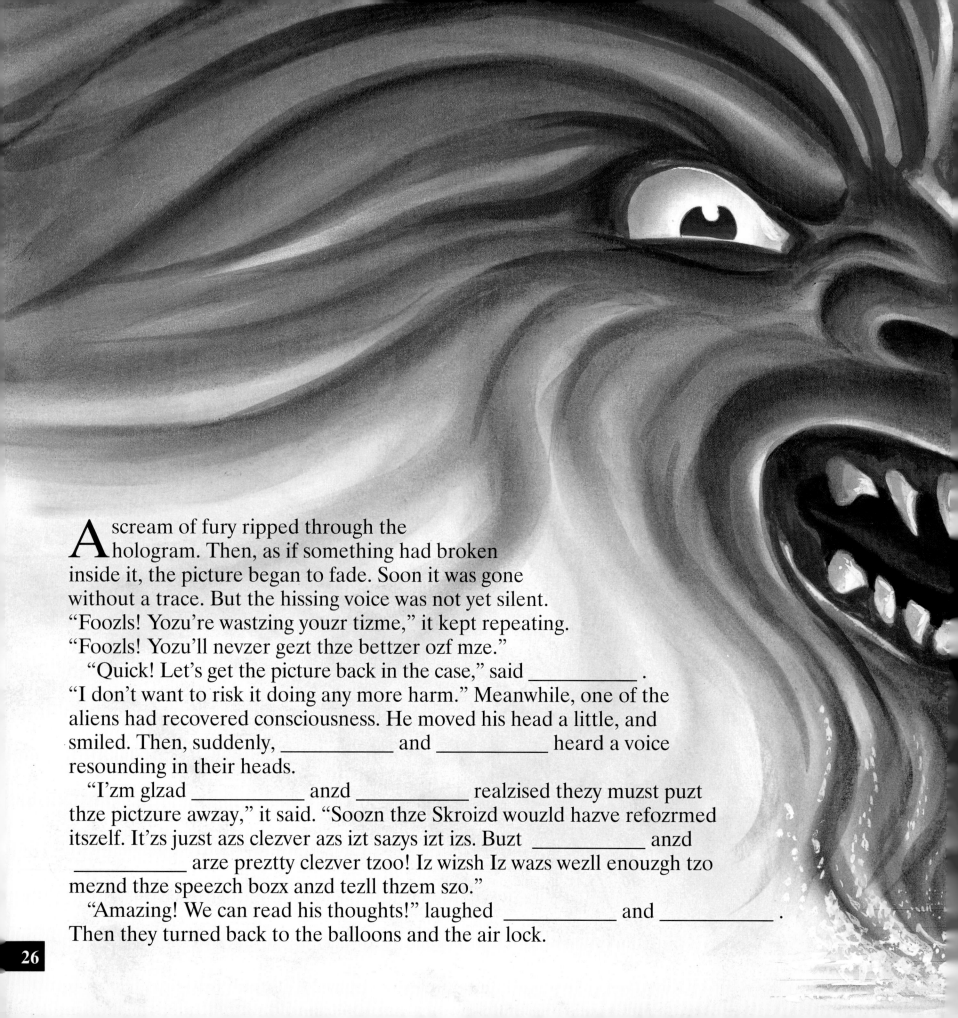

A scream of fury ripped through the hologram. Then, as if something had broken inside it, the picture began to fade. Soon it was gone without a trace. But the hissing voice was not yet silent. "Foozls! Yozu're wastzing youzr tizme," it kept repeating. "Foozls! Yozu'll nevzer gezt thze bettzer ozf mze."

"Quick! Let's get the picture back in the case," said _____. "I don't want to risk it doing any more harm." Meanwhile, one of the aliens had recovered consciousness. He moved his head a little, and smiled. Then, suddenly, _____ and _____ heard a voice resounding in their heads.

"I'zm glzad _____ anzd _____ realzised thezy muzst puzt thze pictzure awzay," it said. "Soozn thze Skroizd wouzld hazve refozrmed itszelf. It'zs juzst azs clezver azs izt sazys izt izs. Buzt _____ anzd _____ arze preztty clezver tzoo! Iz wizsh Iz wazs wezll enouzgh tzo meznd thze speezch bozx anzd tezll thzem szo."

"Amazing! We can read his thoughts!" laughed _____ and _____. Then they turned back to the balloons and the air lock.

The work was now proceeding faster. But there were still holes large enough to let a spaceship through. Relentlessly, the Skroids were getting closer, firing explosives at the B-9 Force ship as they came. _____ and _____ fumbled with the ozone pellets in their haste.

What if they were hit before they could finish their work? The Skroids had seen the rapidly closing holes, and, even now, were racing toward one.

_____ and _____ made a last frantic effort. One sick B-9 alien was crawling to put his hand on the thought-controlled panel. His face contorted with effort. With a mighty push, he managed to turn the spaceship. It swerved, stirring the ozone into a wave that filled a hole.

The Skroids's spaceships shuddered, as they tried to escape the wall of killing ozone, and they released more vengeful shots.

Watching the oncoming missiles, _____ and _____ at last heard clearly what was in the aliens' minds, and knew why they had been chosen for this quest.

According to the aliens, _____ and _____ were the bravest people in the world. Previously, their courage had never had a chance to show itself. The B-9 Force, searching for the help that only human beings could give, had looked into their minds, and had recognized the courage that was there. Suddenly, an enemy missile struck. Everything shattered around them, and _____ and _____ began to fall…

When _____ and _____ woke up, it was morning. They were lying in their own front yard sheltered by the hedge. The sky was blue and calm. Each had a burst balloon clutched in one hand.

Two now familiar voices spoke to them in their heads. The loss of the spaceship, said the aliens, did not matter. The B-9 Force could travel safely without it. The spaceship had simply been necessary for _____ and _____ to travel, and to carry the pellets. The B-9 Force had now returned to Mandria by their normal means of travel. "I wonder how they do that!" thought _____ .

As _____ and _____ crept indoors, they heard the kitchen radio. "Scientists now believe that the recent disturbances in the sky were caused by a meteor. There is no further cause for concern. But, strangely, there appear to be some changes in the ozone layer, entirely for the good."

Mom spotted _____ and _____ as they tried to edge unnoticed through the kitchen door. "You look as if you've been out of bed for hours!" she exclaimed. "What on earth have you been up to?"

_____ and _____ looked at each other, and saw far, far into each other's minds.

"Should we tell her it was not on Earth?" they thought, one to the other.